This book
belongs to

Jodie May Adder

Disney's POCAHONTAS

MOUSE WORKS

ISBN: 1-57082-114-3
10 9 8 7 6 5 4 3 2

The dock around the proud ship *Susan Constant* was buzzing with activity, for this was the day she and her hardy crew of settlers would sail on a dangerous expedition from London to the New World.

Three crew members — Lon, Ben, and Thomas — bid their families tearful farewells before boarding the ship. Another, John Smith, stood alone on deck, impatient for the ship to be on its way.

The last person to appear was John Ratcliffe, the ruthless
and ambitious governor of the New World. In his polished
leather boots he strode onto the boat. Close behind the haughty
Ratcliffe was his enthusiastic and ever-cheerful manservant
Wiggins, carrying Ratcliffe's snooty and spoiled pug dog Percy.
Soon the *Susan Constant* had set sail and was on its way.

After many months at sea, the ship was caught in a terrible storm. One huge wave crashed over the deck, and John Smith's friend Thomas was unable to hold on. He was swept overboard like a tiny doll.

"Hang on, Thomas!" Smith called into the howling wind. And as the rest of the crew on deck watched, frozen in horror, the brave John Smith quickly secured a rope to his waist and jumped into the turbulent water. Moments later, he and Thomas were hauled to safety.

Hearing the commotion, Ratcliffe appeared on deck. "Don't lose heart, men!" he told them. "It won't be long before we reach the New World. And remember what awaits us there. Freedom! Prosperity! And nothing, not even a band of bloodthirsty Indians, shall stand in our way!" With that, Ratcliffe returned to his cabin.

"Just leave the Indians to me. . ." John Smith smiled.

"You think they'll give us much trouble?" Lon asked.

"Not as much trouble as Smith'll give them!" declared Ben.

Across the Atlantic, unaware that the *Susan Constant* was making her way toward them, a party of Indian warriors was returning home from battle. At the tribal village the learned medicine man Kekata, and the rest of the tribe greeted noble Powhatan, their leader, and Kocoum, their bravest young warrior. Powhatan anxiously scanned the welcoming throng for his beloved daughter.

As usual, Pocahontas was off on an adventure with her two mismatched sidekicks: Meeko, an inquisitive raccoon, and a protective hummingbird named Flit. Graceful and quick, the free-spirited young woman stood atop her favorite cliff beside the waterfall. As she gazed out over the breathtaking landscape, her best friend Nakoma called to her from a canoe below.

"Come down here, Pocahontas! Your father is back!"

Pocahontas leapt off the cliff to join her friend, with a startled Meeko and an unhappy Flit tumbling after her.

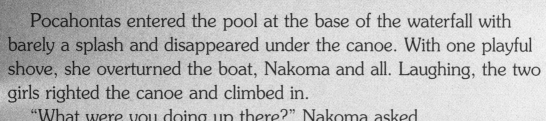

Pocahontas entered the pool at the base of the waterfall with barely a splash and disappeared under the canoe. With one playful shove, she overturned the boat, Nakoma and all. Laughing, the two girls righted the canoe and climbed in.

"What were you doing up there?" Nakoma asked.

"Thinking about that dream again. I know it means something, I just don't know what," Pocahontas said.

"Maybe you should ask your father about it," Nakoma suggested.

"You're right," Pocahontas told her friend. "Let's go!"

15

As soon as she and Powhatan were reunited, Pocahontas told her father about her dream, which told her something exciting was about to happen. A smile crept across her father's face.

"Something exciting *is* about to happen," he said. "Kocoum has asked to seek your hand in marriage."

Pocahontas couldn't believe her ears. Though Kocoum was a mighty warrior, he was too serious, and certainly not someone Pocahontas pictured herself married to.

"But Father," Pocahontas protested. "I think my dream is pointing me down another path."

In reply, Powhatan gave his daughter the necklace her mother had worn at their wedding many years before. As he placed it around her neck, he told her, "Even the wild mountain stream must someday join the big, steady river."

Later, Pocahontas told Meeko, "He wants me to be steady as the river, but to me, it's not steady at all. It's always moving, and around each bend in the river is something new and exciting."

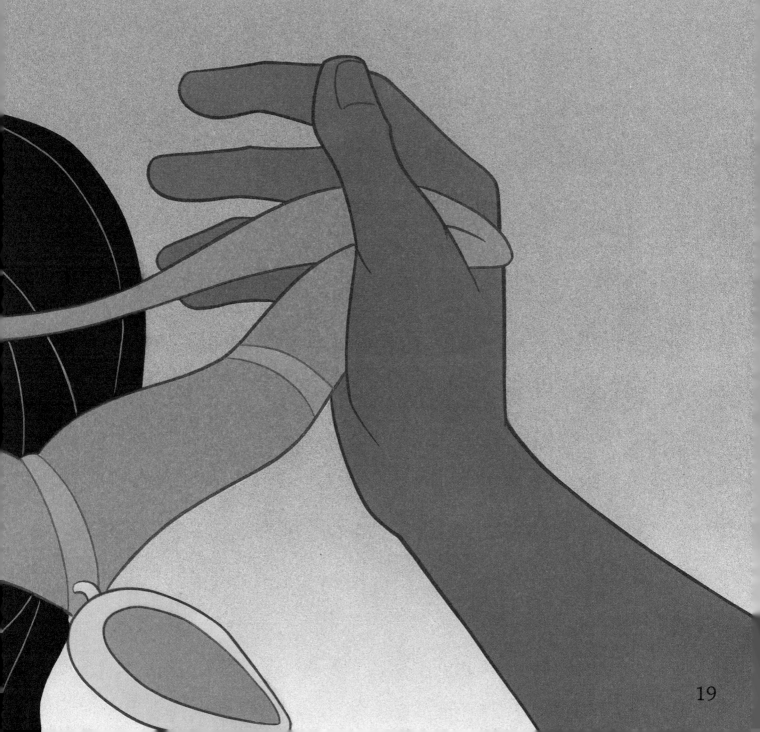

19

Deep in thought, Pocahontas went to a very special glade in the forest inhabited by Grandmother Willow, a magical and wise tree. The Indian maiden told her enchanted friend about her dream.

"I am running through the woods," began Pocahontas, "and then, right there in front of me, is an arrow. It spins faster and faster until suddenly, it stops! Then I wake up. What does it mean, Grandmother Willow?"

"Well, it seems to me this spinning arrow is pointing you down your path," the old tree replied.

"But what is my path? How am I ever going to find it?" continued Pocahontas.

"Your mother asked me the very same question. I told her to listen," Grandmother Willow went on. "All around you are spirits, child. They live in the earth, the water, the sky. If you listen, they will guide you."

Just then a breeze began to blow, picking up speed. Pocahontas climbed high into Grandmother Willow's branches, trying to hear what the wind might be telling her. As she looked out over the trees, she saw clouds billowing in the distance — strange white clouds.

Back aboard the *Susan Constant*, the crew was ready to land, and Ratcliffe gave John Smith special instructions.

"I'm counting on you to make sure that any Indians we find won't disrupt our mission," Ratcliffe told him.

"Don't worry, sir," Smith replied, as he ruffled Percy's fur. "If they're anything like the ones I've fought before, it's nothing I can't handle."

As the ship eased into the shore, Pocahontas was climbing a rock face not far from the water's edge. Though she knew the forest and the waters of her home well, this was a sight she had never before seen. There, much closer now, were the strange "clouds" she had seen earlier — they were really the sails of the *Susan Constant* flapping in the breeze.

The settlers struggled to
pull the ship in and drop the
anchor, but one crew member
was missing. John Smith was
already on the shore, climbing
a tall tree to get a better look at
this magnificent land.

As he climbed, he got closer to Pocahontas's hiding place on the cliff. Though Flit was worried about the stranger's approach, Meeko couldn't wait to meet him. Before Pocahontas could stop him, the mischievous little raccoon darted out into view.

"Well, you're a strange-looking fellow!" Smith said as he held a biscuit out to Meeko. As Meeko gobbled down the treat, he looked back triumphantly to where Pocahontas and Flit were hidden. Smith was just about to investigate when Flit burst out of the bushes, zipping to and fro to distract the stranger.

Just then a bugle sounded from below, calling Smith back to the ship. Pocahontas remained undiscovered — at least for now.

Smith arrived just in time to watch Ratcliffe ceremoniously plant the British flag on the shore. Secretly, Ratcliffe didn't care much about King James and glory for his native England. What he did care about were the gold and other riches this new land had to offer. Just to make sure nothing would get in his way, Ratcliffe sent Smith out to scout the forest for Indians.

The Indian village council was in a heated discussion.
A party of warriors had seen the pale settlers, and now
Powhatan asked Kekata to reveal what their arrival meant.
The medicine man threw a handful of powder into the fire.
The smoke that rose from the flames first took the shape
of armored warriors with weapons spouting fire and
thunder. Then they changed into hungry wolves.

Powhatan was cautious. "Take some men to the river
to observe these white visitors. Let us hope they do not
intend to stay," he told Kocoum.

As he scouted further in the forest, John Smith sensed that he was not alone. Thinking he had gone, Pocahontas crept down from her hiding place as Smith cautiously edged closer to a nearby waterfall. Unable to see the figure on the opposite side of the cascading water, Smith jumped through the falls with his gun aimed directly at her. The startled pair stared at each other for a long moment — and in that lingering moment, their two souls touched. Smith reached out his hand to the lovely young woman before him.

"No, wait, please . . ." he called as Pocahontas darted away.

Smith trailed Pocahontas back to the river. "It's all right, I'm not going to hurt you," he assured her as she climbed into her canoe. "I'm John Smith. What is your name?"

As Smith held out his hand, a light breeze swirled around them, and Pocahontas remembered what Grandmother Willow had told her — to listen with her heart to the voices all around her.

She allowed the pale stranger to help her out of the canoe, and when they touched, neither one wanted to let go.

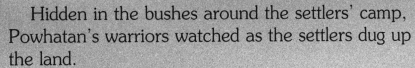

Hidden in the bushes around the settlers' camp, Powhatan's warriors watched as the settlers dug up the land.

"We must find gold!" Ratcliffe ordered. He took one bite of a juicy drumstick and tossed it into the bushes. Percy saw the drumstick land near one of the Indians. His startled yelp sent the settlers scurrying for their guns. In the confrontation that followed, a brave warrior, Namontack, was shot in the leg.

The chief looked at the wounded Namontack and his anger grew. He instructed Kocoum to gather warriors from every village to fight the new enemy.

Powhatan stepped outside and addressed the villagers. "These white men are dangerous!" he said. "No one is to go near them!"

At the river, Pocahontas and John Smith talked, slowly getting to know each other. Meeko reached into Smith's pouch and snatched his compass, thinking it was a biscuit!

As they spoke, Pocahontas shared some of her people's ways with Smith. She showed him the Indian gestures for "hello" and then "good-bye."

"Let's stick with 'hello,'" Smith told her.

As Smith spoke of London, Pocahontas realized that these settlers meant to re-create their old world here among her people. "There is so much we can teach you," concluded Smith. "We've improved the lives of savages all over the world."

Pocahontas glared. "*Savages?*" John Smith fumbled for the right words. "Uh, not that you're a savage. . ."

"Just my people," said Pocahontas.

"Well, what I actually mean," Smith continued feebly, "is *uncivilized*. . . ."

"What you mean is, not like *you*," Pocahontas said coolly.

Before he could protest, Pocahontas took Smith by the hand and led him through the forest. As they ran through the trees, Pocahontas showed him how all the parts of nature — animals, plants, the wind, the clouds, even people — are alive and connected to each other. Her words and the importance of what she showed him so touched his heart that Smith was changed. He could see the colors of the wind that Pocahontas saw, and feel what Pocahontas felt.

Drums echoing through the forest ended their magical time together. "Something's wrong at the village!" Pocahontas said as she ran for home before Smith could say another word.

Later on at the settlement, Ratcliffe was in a rage. Since his men had found no gold, he was sure the Indians had it all. All Smith could think about was Pocahontas.

While Ratcliffe fretted, the always-hungry Meeko sneaked into the tent to steal food from Percy's elaborate dinner plate. Percy spotted him, and the two dashed out of the settlement past the palisade wall the men were building to protect them from the natives.

The Indian warriors were also erecting a palisade wall to protect their village from the settlers. Powhatan warned Pocahontas to stay inside the wall. Then he gazed fondly at his daughter and said, "When I see you wear that necklace, you look just like your mother."

"I wish she was here," Pocahontas answered.

"But she is still with us," replied her father. "Whenever the wind moves through the trees, I feel her presence."

Later, as Pocahontas and Nakoma gathered corn nearby, John Smith emerged from the woods.

"Please don't say anything," Pocahontas begged Nakoma, as she took Smith's hand and disappeared into the forest.

Soon the two arrived at the enchanted glade.
"To think we came all this way just to dig it up
for gold," Smith said.
"What is gold?" Pocahontas asked. After Smith
explained, Pocahontas told him the startling truth:
There was plenty of golden corn to eat, but no gold.

Suddenly they heard a voice, and Grandmother Willow revealed herself in the bark of the old tree. Smith was startled.

"Hello, John Smith," Grandmother Willow said.

"Pocahontas, that tree is talking to me," said the shaken John Smith.

"Don't be frightened, young man," the old tree quipped. "My bark is worse than my bite."

Within minutes, Smith and Grandmother Willow
were chatting like old friends, and Pocahontas knew
that Grandmother Willow approved of her new friend.

Their conversation was interrupted by a voice. "Smith! Where are you, mate?" cried Ben as he and Lon came through the forest. Pocahontas and Smith ducked behind Grandmother Willow.

"This place gives me the creeps," said Lon. "Savages could be hiding anywhere."

They were about to spot Smith when Grandmother Willow gently raised up one of her roots and tripped Lon, sending the two Englishmen scurrying away in fear.

John Smith prepared to return to the camp.

"Meet me tonight. Right here," said Smith.

"I'll be waiting," Pocahontas said, staring deeply into his eyes.

"I should just stay in the village and forget about him," Pocahontas said to Grandmother Willow. "But still, something inside is telling me it's the right thing."

"Perhaps it's your dream," Grandmother Willow suggested.

"My dream!" Pocahontas cried. "Do you think he's the one the spinning arrow was pointing to?"

Grandmother Willow smiled. "Maybe you've found your path, child." Pocahontas thought about these words as she made her way home.

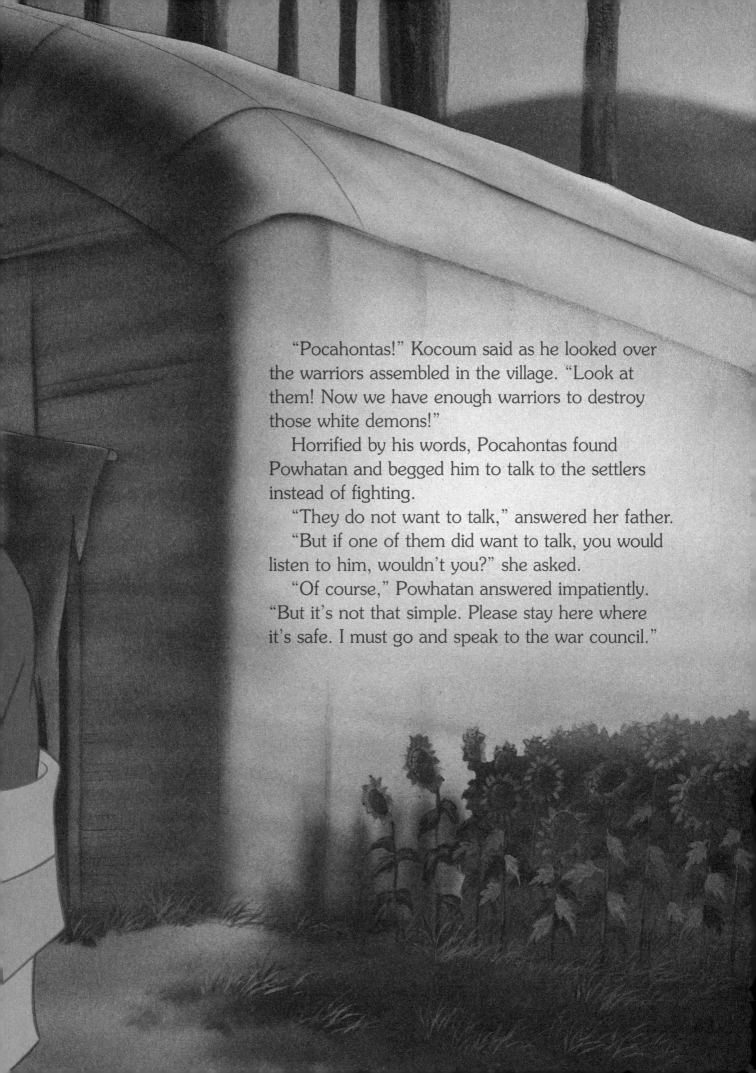

"Pocahontas!" Kocoum said as he looked over the warriors assembled in the village. "Look at them! Now we have enough warriors to destroy those white demons!"

Horrified by his words, Pocahontas found Powhatan and begged him to talk to the settlers instead of fighting.

"They do not want to talk," answered her father.

"But if one of them did want to talk, you would listen to him, wouldn't you?" she asked.

"Of course," Powhatan answered impatiently. "But it's not that simple. Please stay here where it's safe. I must go and speak to the war council."

When Smith arrived at the settlement, Ratcliffe was waiting.

"Prepare the men for battle!" he ordered. "We are going to eliminate these savages once and for all. Then the gold will be ours for the taking!"

Smith tried to convince Ratcliffe that there was no gold. He even brought back an ear of corn, explaining that the Indians had food that would make a welcome change from biscuits and gruel, but Ratcliffe would hear none of it.

"Anyone who so much as looks at an Indian without killing him on sight will be tried for treason and hanged!" he declared.

That night, as Pocahontas crept through the village on her way to meet Smith, Nakoma surprised her at the palisade wall.

"Pocahontas!" cried Nakoma. "You can't go to him. He's one of them! You're turning your back on your own people."

"I'm trying to help my people," she said, as she slipped into the woods. But she could see that her friend did not understand. Nakoma was worried for Pocahontas's safety, so she told Kocoum where Pocahontas had gone.

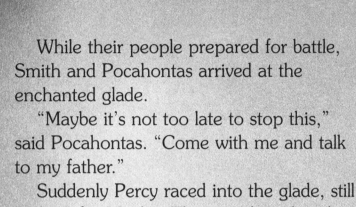

While their people prepared for battle, Smith and Pocahontas arrived at the enchanted glade.

"Maybe it's not too late to stop this," said Pocahontas. "Come with me and talk to my father."

Suddenly Percy raced into the glade, still looking for Meeko. The two chased each other around the glade as Smith and Pocahontas tried to separate them.

"Once two sides want to fight, nothing can stop them," Smith said sadly.

Just then Grandmother Willow dipped one of her branches into the water. "Look, the ripples," she said to Smith. "So small at first, then look how they grow — but someone has to start them."

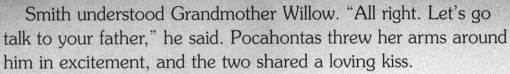

Smith understood Grandmother Willow. "All right. Let's go talk to your father," he said. Pocahontas threw her arms around him in excitement, and the two shared a loving kiss.

At that moment Kocoum emerged from the forest. He pulled the couple apart and leapt at Smith. They wrestled for control of Kocoum's knife.

Suddenly, Thomas appeared out of the bushes to see Kocoum with his dagger poised above Smith's body. Thomas fired his musket, fatally wounding the brave warrior. As Kocoum fell, his hand caught on the necklace Pocahontas was to wear at their wedding, and it fell to the ground near his lifeless body.

"Thomas, get out of here!" yelled Smith as a party of warriors descended on them. Pocahontas watched in disbelief as Smith was dragged away, accused of being Kocoum's murderer.

Back at the village Powhatan condemned Smith to die at sunrise the next day. When Pocahontas protested, her father's words were harsh.

"Because of your foolishness, Kocoum is dead," he told her. "You have shamed your father!"

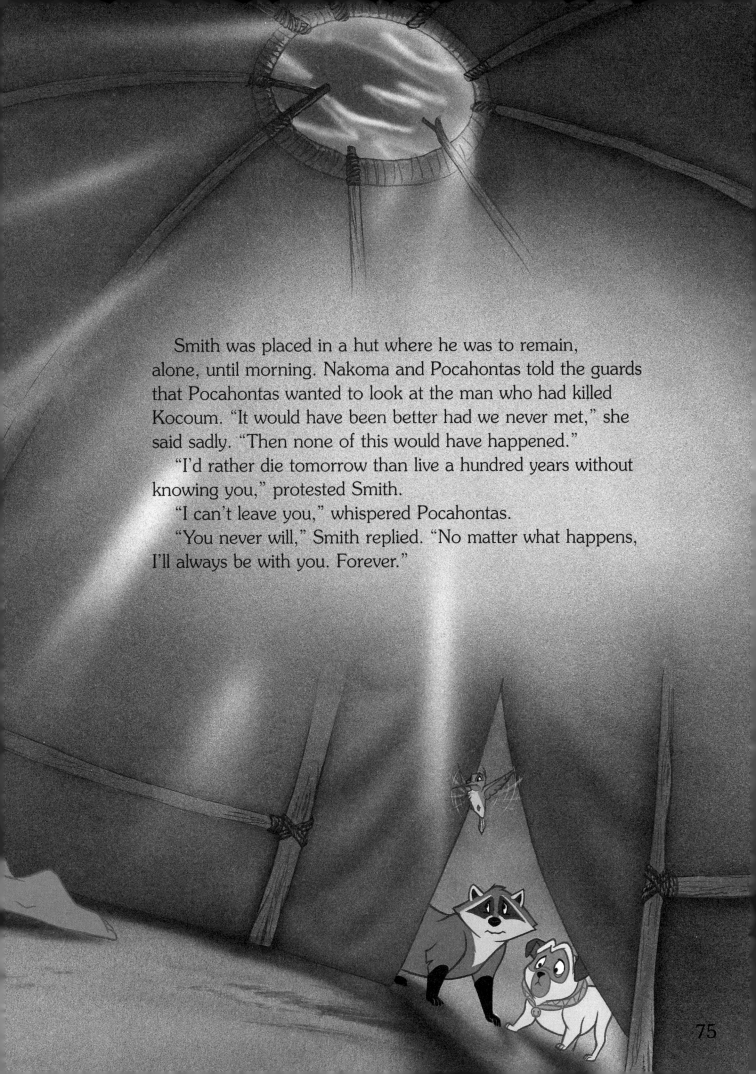

Smith was placed in a hut where he was to remain, alone, until morning. Nakoma and Pocahontas told the guards that Pocahontas wanted to look at the man who had killed Kocoum. "It would have been better had we never met," she said sadly. "Then none of this would have happened."

"I'd rather die tomorrow than live a hundred years without knowing you," protested Smith.

"I can't leave you," whispered Pocahontas.

"You never will," Smith replied. "No matter what happens, I'll always be with you. Forever."

Meanwhile, Thomas raced back to the settlement as fast as his legs would carry him. "The savages!" he screamed as he reached the clearing. "They've captured Smith!"

"You see?" said Ratcliffe. "Smith tried to befriend them and look what they've done to him. I say it's time to kill them all and rescue our courageous comrade!"

Pocahontas drifted into the enchanted glade, her head hung in sadness. Just then Meeko handed her John Smith's compass. As she took it, something amazing happened: its arrow was spinning and she knew it was the sign from her dream. "I have to go back," she said excitedly. Suddenly the arrow stopped. Pocahontas looked where it pointed and saw the morning light. "The sunrise! It's too late! What can I do?"

"Let the spirits of the earth guide you," urged Grandmother Willow.

The settlers, armed and ready for war with the Indians, marched through the forest like an angry army. At the same time, the Indians moved in a fateful procession toward the execution site. They could not know that the settlers were nearing the cliff. It seemed that nothing could stop these enemies from a violent clash.

Atop the cliff, the warriors placed Smith's head on a large stone slab. Just as Powhatan raised his club to deliver the fatal blow, the settlers burst through the woods, ready to open fire.

Suddenly, Pocahontas appeared and threw herself over Smith. "No," she shouted. "If you kill him, you'll have to kill me too! Look around you. This is where the path of hatred has brought us!" As everyone stared in stunned silence, Pocahontas said, "You have the power to change that, Father."

The wind swirled, and Powhatan felt the spirit of Pocahontas's mother guiding him to hear with his heart and heed the wisdom of his daughter's words. "Pocahontas speaks with courage and understanding," he said. "From this day forward there will be no more killing. Let us be guided instead to a place of peace."

The Indian warriors put down their weapons uncertainly. "Now's our chance, men!" yelled Ratcliffe. "Fire!"

But the settlers finally understood the governor's greed, and one by one they lowered their muskets. Ratcliffe desperately grabbed a gun and fired at Powhatan.

The brave John Smith threw himself in front of the chief and knocked Powhatan out of the way. But the bullet meant for the Indian caught Smith instead. The settlers were enraged.

"Get him!" shouted Ben as he, Lon, and Thomas lunged at Ratcliffe. The governor was quickly put in chains and taken back to the ship.

John Smith lay on a stretcher as the *Susan Constant* prepared to set sail for England.

Pocahontas appeared at the edge of the clearing. Behind her were Powhatan, Nakoma, and the rest of the village, bearing blankets and corn for the settlers.

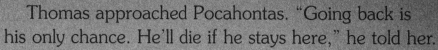

Thomas approached Pocahontas. "Going back is his only chance. He'll die if he stays here," he told her.

Pocahontas knelt by Smith's side. "Here," she said, handing him a small pouch. "It's from Grandmother Willow's bark. It will help with the pain."

Powhatan approached and placed his cloak over Smith's body. "You are always welcome among our people. Thank you, my brother," he said softly.

Just then Meeko, Flit, and Percy arrived. They carried with them her mother's necklace, which they lovingly placed around Pocahontas's neck.

Smith looked up at Pocahontas. "Come with me?" he asked.

Pocahontas turned to her father.

"You must choose your own path," he said.
But as Pocahontas watched the Indians sharing baskets
of food with the hungry settlers in the first signs of peace
between them, she knew what her path must be.

"Pocahontas, the fighting stopped because of you. If you
leave. . ." Nakoma begged.

Her tears told John Smith better than words ever could what Pocahontas had decided. She would stay and help forge a bond between her people and the settlers. "Then I'll stay with you," Smith whispered.

"No, you have to go back," Pocahontas answered. "No matter what happens, I will always be with you. Forever." Then Pocahontas leaned down and the two gently shared their last kiss.

Pocahontas watched as John Smith was placed into a dinghy and rowed away. Choking back the tears, Pocahontas placed her head on Powhatan's shoulder as he tried to comfort her.

Smith was lifted onto the ship, and the sails of the *Susan Constant* unfurled in the breeze. Pocahontas broke away from her father's embrace and disappeared into the forest.

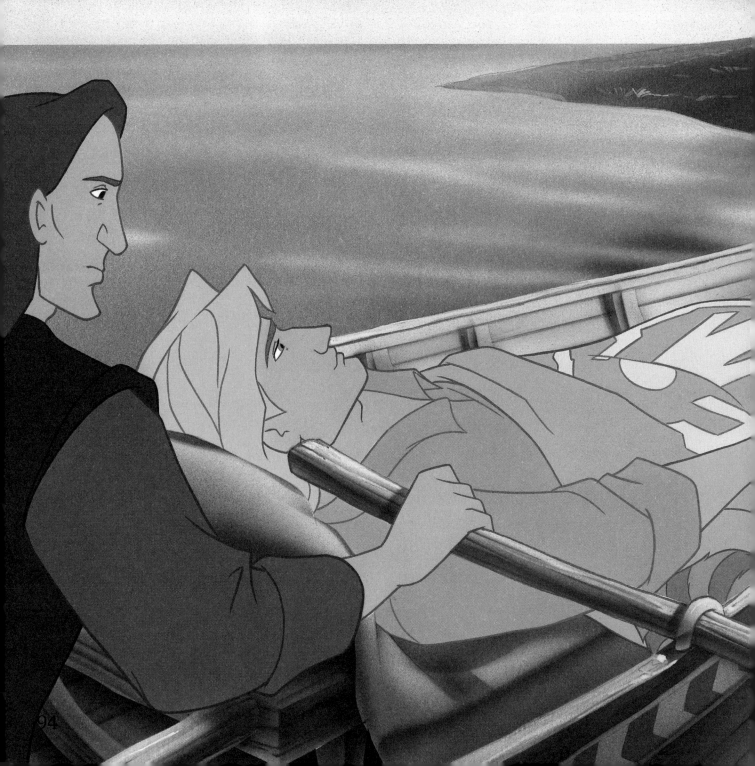

Steadfast Pocahontas stood atop her favorite cliff, the wind swirling around her. She watched as that same wind carried the ship that bore John Smith down the river and out to the open sea.